In memory of Anna Herttrich
1915–2011

ORCHARD BOOKS
Carmelite House
50 Victoria Embankment
London EC4Y 0DZ

First published in 2013 by Orchard Books
First published in paperback in 2014

ISBN 978 1 40832 634 3

A CIP catalogue record for this book is available from the British Library.

9 10 8

Printed in China

Orchard Books
An imprint of Hachette Children's Group
Part of The Watts Publishing Group Limited
An Hachette UK Company
www.hachette.co.uk

THE MEMORY TREE

BRITTA TECKENTRUP

ORCHARD

There was once a fox who lived with all the other animals in the forest.

Fox had lived a long and happy life, but now he was tired.
Very slowly, Fox made his way to his favourite spot in the clearing.
He looked at his beloved forest one last time and lay down.
Fox closed his eyes,

took a deep breath

and fell asleep

forever.

Everything around Fox was still and peaceful.

Snow began to fall, gently covering him with a soft blanket.

Owl had watched Fox from the top of his tree.

He flew down and landed next to his friend.

Owl was very sad.

He had known Fox for a long time.

But Owl knew the time had come for his friend to leave.

One by one, Fox's friends came to the clearing.

First Squirrel and Weasel, then Bear, Deer and Bird and, finally,

Rabbit, Mouse and others came to sit by Fox.

Fox had been loved by everyone. He had been kind and caring.

No one could imagine life in the forest without him.

The animals sat in silence for a very long time.

Owl was the first to speak.

He smiled warmly and said, "I remember when Fox and I
were very young. Every autumn, we raced to see who
could catch more falling leaves."

The other animals remembered and smiled.

Mouse said softly, "I remember how much Fox
loved the sunset. He always sat at this exact spot."

The animals remembered. Many of them had
joined Fox, watching the sun go down.

It was a happy memory, and their sad hearts filled with warmth.

Bear remembered how Fox had looked after her cubs one spring.

Rabbit smiled when she told the story of how
Fox had played tag with her in the tall grass.

Squirrel talked about Fox helping him dig up
buried nuts in the deep snow last winter.

One by one, the animals remembered their
favourite stories about Fox.

Fox had touched the lives of all the animals in the forest with his
warmth and kindness, and they all smiled, remembering.

While the animals talked, a little orange plant grew out
of the snow where Fox was lying.
Small and delicate at first, and hardly noticeable,
the plant grew bigger, stronger and more beautiful with each story.

The animals talked about Fox all through the night.

And, in the morning, the little plant had grown into

a small tree.

The animals saw the tree and knew that

Fox was still a part of them.

During the next days, weeks and months,
the animals remembered many more stories about Fox.

Their heavy hearts began to feel lighter.

The more they remembered, the more the tree
grew, higher and higher and more and more beautiful,
until it was the tallest tree in the forest. A tree made from
memories and full of love.

Fox's tree was big and strong enough to shelter all the animals. It was always buzzing with life. The birds built their nests among the leaves and Owl raised his grandchicks on the branches. Squirrel found a cosy home in the trunk and Bear, Deer and Rabbit slept in its shade. The tree gave strength to everyone who had loved Fox.

And so, Fox lived on in their hearts forever.